Hi, Parents!

Your child's love of reading starts here, with HarperAlley's **I Can Read Comics**!

I Can Read Comics introduces children to the world of graphic novel storytelling and encourages visual literacy in emerging readers. Comics inspire reader engagement unlike any other format. They ask readers to infer and answer questions, like:

1. What do I read first? Image or text?
2. Why is this word balloon shaped this way, and that word balloon shaped that way?
3. Why is a character making that facial expression? Are they happy, angry, excited, sad?

From the comics your child reads with you to the first comic they read on their own, there are **I Can Read Comics** for every stage of reading:

LEVEL 1

Simple stories for shared reading.

LEVEL 2

Engaging stories for children reading on their own.

LEVEL 3

Complex stories for independent readers.

The magic of graphic novel storytelling lies between the gutters. Unlock the magic with…

I Can Read Comics!

Visit **ICanRead.com** for information on enriching your child's reading experience.

I Can Read *Comics* Cartooning Basics

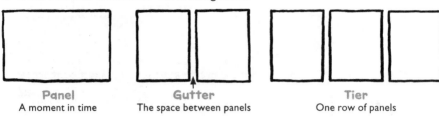

Panel	**Gutter**	**Tier**
A moment in time	The space between panels	One row of panels

Word Balloons When someone talks, thinks, whispers, or screams, their words go in here:

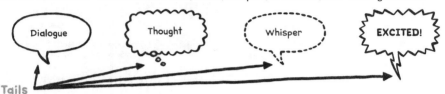

Dialogue Thought Whisper EXCITED!

Tails
Point to whoever is talking / thinking / whispering / screaming / etc.

A quick how-to-read comics guide:

In a **panel**, read the text on the **left** first.

Then, read the text on the **right**.

Remember to...
Read the text along with the image, paying close attention to the character's acting, the action, and/or the scene. Every little detail matters!

No dialogue? No problem!
If there is no dialogue within a panel, take the time to read the image. Visual cues are just as important as text, so don't forget about them!

On a page, **start here**, in the **top left** corner!

After that, read the panel immediately to the **right**.

When you're done up there, come down here and read **this** panel next!

ME NEXT! ME NEXT!

You're almost there...

YOU MADE IT! You just read a comic page!

YAY!

To Eje, Kim, Sharlae, and Jan for all our school music-making —B.H.

To my sixth grade teacher, Mr. Wilson —G.F.

HarperAlley is an imprint of HarperCollins Publishers.
I Can Read® and I Can Read Book® are trademarks of HarperCollins Publishers.

Clark the Shark and the School Sing

Library of Congress Control Number: 2020952906
ISBN 978-0-06-291257-2 (trade bdg.) — ISBN 978-0-06-291256-5 (pbk.)

Book design by Chrisila Maida
23 24 CWM 10 9 8 7 6 5 4 3   ❖   First Edition

I Can Read! Comics

LEVEL 1

CLARK THE SHARK
AND THE SCHOOL SING

By **BRUCE HALE** Pictures by **GUY FRANCIS**

HARPER alley

An Imprint of HarperCollins Publishers

7

When Clark got home...

If you're happy and you know it, clap your fins!

The next day, at school...

16

And every day,
the same result.

Finally the big day arrived!

But when the kids looked out at the audience, they froze.

The end.